Floating Away

(Tales of Endings, Change and Beginnings)

These tales are taken from my books
'A Curious Book (Dark)' and 'A
Curious Book (Light)

The Mother who couldn't say Goodbye

Once upon a time… many, many years ago in a world long since forgotten, there was a country called Anywhere. And in the land of Anywhere there was a fine and prosperous city called Anyplace and within the city of Anyplace was a hospital for children. In a particular room in this hospital lay a particular child, a boy of just nine years of age. The Boy had been struck down by one of the cruellest threads that the Blind Old Weaver Of Fate, in all her capricious randomness, can weave. The Boy was dying of an Incurable Cancer.

Sitting with The Boy was his Mother, She sat, still, determined, watchful for The Boy's doctors had told him that the ravages of the Incurable Cancer were now such that this day would Most Likely be The Boy's Last Day and The Mother was determined not to miss a moment for she loved The Boy absolutely, this child was her life, she had seen him into this world and held him in his first few seconds of his life; she would see him out of this world, too, and hold him in his *last* few seconds of life.

As The Mother sat in her Patient Vigil over her dying

son, she thought briefly of The Boy's father. It was sad he was not here; he had been a handsome but Selfish and Self-Obsessed man and had abandoned his wife and son in the second year of The Boy's life to Take Up With another woman, a Younger Model. Not once had he ever contacted wife and son again and The Mother knew not where he was. Ever since his departure it had been her and The Boy. Everything she did for The Boy, her horrible, poorly paid job, the long hours, the worries about rents and bills, the sheer bloody struggle of everyday life for an Ordinary Person in this land where once again The Greedy One Percent were in Rapacious Ascendancy...that, all of that, it was all for The Boy and it was all made worthwhile by The Boy. Everything for The Boy because The Boy is Everything. Such is the Nature Of Love.

The Mother reaches out a hand, across The Boy's bed, and lays it on her son's forehead. The Boy moves slightly and, to The Mother's delight, a smile blossoms on his pale face. A feeling of warmth travels up The Mother's arm and she feels blessed relief from the Howling Horror of her and The Boy's sorry circumstances. And suddenly a picture forms in her mind, of an expanse of fields and woodland, an isolated rural area many miles outside Anyplace that she and The Boy had visited many times; The Boy had loved it there and as he ran through the grass and flowers, dodging in and out of trees, radiant and healthy under a Broad, Bright Blue Sky he would excitedly ask Mum, Will We See a Troll, Will We See A Troll?

And in The Mother's head, as real as you are sitting there reading this, The Boy speaks and says, Please Mum, Not Here Mum, Not In This Cold, White Room.

Suddenly all is clear. The Mother knows that this is not the place her son should die. Not here, not here in this bureaucratically nondescript cell, surrounded by the Professional Indifference of doctors and nurses and by the Tragedy of Too Many Other young lives fading far too soon into The Dense Fog Of Forgotten Stories. Her son shall die in that place of grass and flowers that he loves so much, that place so open to the Possibilities of the Broad, Bright Blue Sky.

So it was that The Mother gathered up The Boy to herself and took him from that cold, white place. It should have been a difficult thing to steal away a dying child from a hospital but God, in one of his rare moments of actually Paying Attention to what was going on in one of The Many Worlds He Had Created, was moved by this Tale of a boy and a mother and intervened with the Blind Old Weaver Of Fate to ensure that some Rare Lucky Threads Of Gold were spun into the story of both The Mother and The Boy. On the way out of the hospital, nobody challenged the woman who was clutching to herself a sick child. Two nurses and an orderly thought briefly of saying something but had a sense of intruding on Something They Did Not Understand and Should Leave Well Alone.

And so The Mother and The Boy passed by nurses, doctors, orderlies unmolested and left the hospital. Outside, a passing clarb driver noticed the pair; a weary and distraught mother holding to her body and heart a pale and obviously very sick child. Moved at a level he at once Understood But Did Not Understand, the clarb driver pulled over and asked The Mother if she would like a lift and where too and There'll Be No Fair To Pay, Darlin'.

Soon they arrived in the hills outside of Anyplace, where resided the Gross And Tasteless Mansions of the vile and destructive Greedy One Percent. The Mother and The Boy took leave of the kind clarb driver and began to walk. They walked past the mansions of the Rapaciously Rapist Rich, over the hills that surrounded Anyplace and out, far, far out into the wild and beautiful countryside that constitutes most of the land of Anywhere. For two hours The Mother walked, carrying The Boy with Love and Care, as if he where The Most Precious Thing In The World. At no time did she stop or lay The Boy down to rest her arms; for her The Boy never became heavy, never became a burden, never made her weary. Whether that be because of the Magick that still lives on in the land of Anywhere or the Simple Power Of Love you must decide for yourself.

At last The Mother and The Boy were deep within the wild, rural landscape which the boy loved so much, a place where few people came and where Magick and Trolls can still be found. Coming to grassy hillock, spotted with beautiful purple and yellow flowers, near a small stand of trees, The Mother sat. She lifted her son, pale and barely breathing, upwards in her arms and held her face to that of the child, pressing cheek to cheek and silently she wept Tears Of Utter Desolation. But as she cried she felt that feeling of warmth she had felt earlier in the hospital and once again her son's voice was in her head. Mum, Thanks For Bringing Me Here, This Is Where I Wanted To Be. Of Course, My Son, Anything For You. It's Beautiful Here, Isn't It, Mum? And Mum, Mum, Guess What…We're Going To Meet A Troll!!

And no sooner had The Boy Uttered these words in The Mother's head then who should emerge from out of the nearby trees? A Troll, that's who. A huge Troll. And one of great age, for this Troll's fur was entirely grey. In no time at all (for even very old Trolls move at great speed) the Troll was standing before The Mother and The Boy. Calmly the Troll sat down in front of the pair. At this point The Mother as was somewhat perturbed, for humans see Trolls as dangerous and violent. In reality, Trolls are gentle, peaceful creatures, charged by The Universe with protecting Love and all that is Good and

Decent, but they have been demonised by The Greedy And Murderous Rich and the Bankers and their tame and controlled Means Of Communication to justify killing them and stealing their lands for Development Purposes.

The Troll, aware what most humans think of his kind, quickly explained all this to The Mother to forestall her fear. He explained that he'd been called to be In This Place At This Time by The Boy and so he had come, for it is a Universal Law that no Troll can ignore the Wishes Of A Dying Child of any species, and The Boy had two wishes for the short time he had left in this world: to meet a Troll and to depart on his Final Journey across a Broad, Bright Blue Sky from the arms of his mother, in a place he had loved so much when he had been well.

The Troll instructed The Mother, now made peaceful and at ease by the Troll's gentle demeanour and calm voice, to look down at The Boy's face. And she did so, and she saw that The Boy was smiling in a way you in your world would call "from ear to ear" and that, more, the pain of illness seemed to have left his face: he looked like a Happy And Healthy Little Boy who was Simply Asleep, an impression added to by the fact The Mother could see that, under The Boy's eyelids, his eyes were darting back and forth mischievously, as though he were having a Happy Dream.

The Mother looked back at the Troll and smiled at him in gratitude. Somehow, she knew not how but she knew, her son's happier state was due to the Troll. The Troll smiled back at the woman and suddenly tilted his huge head to the left, cocking a big Troll ear upwards, as though catching a Whisper On The Breeze.

The Troll looked thoughtful and said to The Mother:

"I hear another Wish flying through the Universe. It is your Wish. It says to me you no longer have a use for this world, that this world without The Boy is an empty place for you, one in which you do not wish to remain. Think carefully, human, if this is what you want, I can make it so for this is still a land of Magick, humans have destroyed much of it for you are its antithesis as the Devil walks amongst you, but it is still there and can still be reached. There are Words, ancient Words, that if uttered will free the Souls of you and your son to make a journey across the Broad, Bright Blue Sky to That Which Lies

Beyond together. Tell me, shall I speak those words?"

The Mother clutched her son even tighter and huge tears welled up in her eyes and there was no need to answer the question.

The Troll began to speak Words. Words from a language that is older than the very genetic code of Humanity. The Words were Deep and Rolling and Rhythmic and Hypnotic. The Mother felt herself slipping away to Another Place, felt as if herself and her son were becoming one and suddenly The Boy's eyes opened and met the Mother's and The Boy laughed and said in a voice that sounded like the Sweetest Music:

"Hey, Mum, it's time for us to go now!"

Together, the Boy and The Mother were cloaked in a bright, white light which grew in intensity and suddenly exploded outwards. And their Souls, Woman and Boy, were simultaneously freed from their Earthly Bodies.

The Souls shot upwards, burning an Incandescent

Path across the Broad, Bright Blue Sky, together performing a dance of burning light, of a complexity as intense and beautiful as the irresistible, flawless logic of a Mathematical Equation or the eye catching wonder of a Murmuration Of Starlings. And occasionally, in the course of their dance across the sky, the two souls would glance off each other and from each meeting would radiate out a huge, circular rainbow of awe-inspiring radiance and such size as to be visible as far away as the city of Anyplace where those that saw it would be moved in a way that they at once Understood But Did Not Understand.

And the motto of this tale is...why, you already know it!...love is all. The rest ain't worth a damn.

The Dog who moved Death to Tears

Once upon a time in the land of Anywhere, in a world long since forgotten, in the fine and prosperous city of Anyplace there lived a man, an older man who had found his life mired in sadness and sameness.

As a child, you see, the man had been a Special Boy. An only child, beloved by his parents and a boy of Great And Unusual Intelligence who liked routine, stability and predictability. He liked numbers. With numbers one plus one was always two, but with people one plus one could be…well, it could be anything. As the boy grew he became more and more happy in the World Of Numbers – the use of which he cultivated to genius level- and less and less happy in the World Of People and others regarded him not as rude or unpleasant, for he was neither of these things, but as slightly odd and withdrawn. Consequently he never developed true, meaningful relationships with others but - thanks to the love, dedication and hard work of his parents - he had at least enough Social Skills drilled into him to Get By.

Indeed, when the boy became the man, he used his dexterity with and love of numbers to build a very successful career in Matters Actuarial.

Sadly, this career success was not matched by relationship success and the man never moved away from the family home, eventually living there alone after both his Loved and Loving parents passed away.

The years, as they do, ticked by and eventually the man reached the Age Of Retirement and, much to his displeasure, had to leave his job.

Soon the man became disillusioned with life. He had lost his parents, the only people he'd ever been able to experience true Companionship with and now he'd lost his job – a job in which he'd revelled in the simple, unambiguous companionship of numbers. A job he'd been good at and had enjoyed. He felt alone, isolated, lost. He felt life had no more to offer him expect empty day following empty day. He felt no more than an observer of a world that was passing him by, a world that he didn't understand and that didn't understand him. A world that didn't need him.

A deep sadness enveloped the man. That sadness grew, malignantly, into a deep depression and each day became a torture to live.

The man decided that the best thing to would be to leave the world and resolved that he would kill himself.

To that end, he locked himself in the bedroom that had been his since childhood. He took with him a sturdy rope and a rickety wooden a chair, a piece of paper and a pencil. Examining chair and rope and distance from ceiling to floor, he quickly sketched out some Freefrom Algorithms to which he applied sine and cosine calculations to produce what he thought was very interesting equation...

Given that:

C = Chair
H = Height
R = Rope
F = Flexibility
D = Drop

Then:

$$H - C \times (R + F) + D = TTD \text{ (Time to Death)}$$

In this fashion, and true to his love of numbers, he worked out the optimum way in which to hang himself (taking into account height from floor to ceiling, size of chair, flexibility of rope, length of drop etc. etc.) to ensure the shortest Time To Death.

Calculations done and checked, he took his length of rope and fastened one end to a sturdy rafter in the bedroom ceiling. The other he fashioned into a noose. He pulled up that rickety chair, slipped his head into the noose, and stepped up...

But...our story is not yet at an end.

For living in the sheds, outhouses and shrubbery of the man's neighbourhood, surviving on scraps, left-overs and occasional charity was an Urban Troll. Now, Urban Trolls were somewhat of a feature of this period in the history of The Land Of Anywhere – a period in which the loathsome Greedy One Percent were once again in the ascendency, their rapacious appetites consuming everything they could lay their scaly, Devil-Driven hands on. Especially land. Land which had been in the possession of Trolls for time immemorial, which the Greedy One Percent and the Banker Class coveted for Redevelopment Purposes. This Policy Of Acquisition had resulted in many homeless Trolls, some of who had gravitated towards Anywhere's urban area, having nowhere else to go. Hence the phenomenon of Urban Trolls.

And whilst humans are usually blind or indifferent to (or worse, take pleasure in) the pain and suffering of others, Trolls are not. Trolls are attuned to the suffering not only of their own kind but of all living creatures; a pre-requisite of their Universe-Given task to preserve All That Is Good And Decent in the world and protect Universal Harmony. Consequently, the Troll had been aware for some time of the pain the man had been experiencing and had a degree of concern for his welfare. On the day the man decided to kill himself, the Troll's Troll Sense had gone into overdrive: she felt (for our particular Troll was a lady Troll) that somewhere near something bad was about to happen and, at the same time as the man put a noose around his neck, this Troll Sense went from overdrive to screaming alarm. She knew exactly what bad thing was going to happen and where! The Troll leapt out of a thick stand of shrubbery in which she had been tucking into a pungent feast of scraps and garbage and ran as fast as her large, incredibly powerful Troll legs would carry her (which is very, very fast indeed).

In a matter of only seconds she was crashing through the front door of the man's house, flying upstairs and smashing through the door to the bedroom, in which she found the man - noose around his neck, perched precariously on a rickety old wooden chair which he was just about to kick away. The man turned, observing from his elevated position that there was a huge Troll with enormous, pendulous breasts in his room (it is a feature of Trolls that humans find vaguely disturbing that the female of the species has very, very large breasts whilst the male of the species is massively well endowed). He barely had time to register his surprise before the Troll had enfolded him in her huge arms, removed the noose from around his neck and plonked him down on the floor to give him a Jolly Good Talking To, as if he were a recalcitrant and naughty child.

The Troll explained to him that his Planned Exit from this life was Premature. No matter how Overwhelmingly Black the threads of his life were at the moment, that blackness would pass: there were still things he had to learn, to do, to experience. Every now and then, as the Troll lectured the man, she would reach out one of her huge hands and, with Tenderness Surprising In A Creature So Huge, smooth down the hair on his head or gently stroke the side of his face.

And the Troll said everything she said to the man with such Warmth and Sincerity and Tenderness and that he Believed Every Word.

Speech over, the Troll bent down, kissed the man on the head and left. The man no longer saw a reason to kill himself, the Troll was right, there were still things to do, life still had things to offer him and he still had things to offer life.

The next day the man decided that what he really, really needed was change, a chance to discover a new way of living. Tired of the city and wishing to escape the Deafening Silence of a home that was now just a house and the presence of people who Did Not Notice Him, he sold up and moved to an isolated log cabin deep in the woods, many miles away from the city of Anyplace and its noise and brashness and people.

There the man developed a quiet, simple way of life, waking when the sun rose and sleeping when it set. He played numerous and innumerable games with numbers, grew his own food, hunting and fishing to supplement his diet. He read and he thought and he walked and gave hospitality (in his own stilted way) to the occasional traveller who was passing through. And this different, quiet way of living was like Balm To His Soul.

One particular day, an hour or so before sunset, the man, on one of his walks, paused at a favourite spot of his: not far from his cabin rose a tall hill, wooded like all around it, and towards the top of this hill was a small, flat area of stone and grass, a clearing from which a magnificent view of the woods below was granted. He would always take a moment to sit in this beautiful spot and reflect on life. Today was no different except, as he sat there, a small furry bundle stumbled out of the surrounding undergrowth and walked towards him before stopping and sitting clumsily down on its behind, head tilted to one side, regarding the man cautiously. The furry bundle was a dog, little more than a puppy, probably a descendant of one of the many, many dogs dumped in the woods over the years, unwanted domestic pets abandoned by thoughtless and irresponsible human owners.

The man looked back at the dog, a ragged ball of brown fur with a bushy tail and pointed, sticky-up ears, and smiled. He made reassuring noises and gestured the dog to 'come' to him but it stayed resolutely in position. The man thought and remembered that in his shoulder bag he had the remains of last night's stew that he'd brought with him, intending to eat it, in fact, in this very place. Perfect! Who's ever met a dog that wasn't hungry!

In this way, a chance meeting and the offering of cold stew, a relationship between a man and a dog began that would last for many years. At that first meeting, after the man had gained the confidence of the dog with his cold stew, he considered scooping up the young dog and taking it back with him to his cabin. But in his heart he knew that this dog was, essentially, a wild thing and it would be better if he did not try to Change Its Nature. Instead, he returned to that spot the next day at the same time, once again bringing food. And once again, the dog was there. And the same again the next day. And the next...

All in all, man and dog would meet at that same place at the same time every day for ten years. Always the man would offer the dog something to eat and the two would sit for an hour or so in companionable silence or the man would talk; he would ask the dog how its day had been, comment on the weather and what he himself had been up to. Often he would talk about his old job or his parents – sometimes this conversation would trail off to silence as though the man were reluctant to talk more, at which point the dog would bark at him in encouragement. Other times, the man's reminiscences of An Earlier Life would bring tears to his eyes and the dog would seek to reassure and comfort the man by sitting in his lap and licking away the tears.

The man looked forward every day to meeting the dog and in time regarded the dog not as a dog but as a Furry Friend and came to love the animal. For the dog had given something he had not had since the death of his mother and father – true Companionship. The dog, too, looked forward every day to his meeting with the man, regarding him, perhaps, as a large, smooth dog or as a friend or, well, who knows exactly what dogs regard people as but, suffice to say, the dog grew to love the man as the man loved the dog.

But everything, good and bad, comes to an end and the day came when the man, who was now an old man, passed away – in his sleep, quietly and peacefully and his last thoughts, before his Soul left his Mortal Shell and journeyed across a Broad, Bright Blue Sky to That Which Lies Beyond, were of his parents and that little dog he'd met ten years before, his Furry Friend.

Later that day, the dog would go to the place where, every day for so long, dog and man had met. The dog waited and waited, stayed in that place until the sun set. But the man did not come. Puzzled and upset, the dog returned to the woods.

The next day, the dog returned to the meeting place. Again the man did not come.

The dog returned faithfully to that little clearing high up a hill the next day and the next and the next. But the man was never there. The dog did not understand why his friend had abandoned him and took to sitting in that spot where he and the man had passed so much time and howling. And every day, an hour before sunset, the dog would return to that spot and sit and howl, and that howl was full of the Pain and Sorrow of Abandonment and such was the emotion it contained that it came to the attention of Faeries (who are drawn to strong emotion as bees to honey) and Trolls and, one day, Death Himself.

Death, you see, is a busy fellow, always on the move, always with appointments to keep. And on that day, Death had several appointments in the general Time and

Space around where the little dog in our tale sat howling. And Death heard that little dog and was moved, like the Faeries and the Trolls, by the Purity Of Pain it held in its Soul…

So Death made a detour from His planned route.

Death, you should understand, has two faces (remember, one of the most profound principles of the Universe is The Duality Of All Things). The first is violent, sudden, premature, unexpected. The second is welcome and merciful. As Death stood, quiet and unseen in front of the dog, it was this second face that came to the fore. For Death saw that the dog was not just howling but crying, shedding real tears from its warm, loving brown eyes. Now Death has been around an awfully long time, but even He had not seen a dog cry, and he was Deeply Moved and even shed tears of his own. He chose to do the one thing of beauty, love and care that Death can do - he reached out his hand and laid it gently on the dog's head. The howling, and tears, came to an end and the dog's Soul slid from its body in Joy And Liberation, burning an incandescent path across a Broad, Bright Blue Sky passing to That Which Lies Beyond where it would forever be reunited with the Soul of the man - two souls dancing together across the Infinite Vastness of The Circle Of Time, coming together and parting (but always, always finding each other) in life after life after life.

And the motto of this tale is: love is a bond that lasts an eternity.

The Old Lady's Story

Once upon a time…many, many years ago in a world long since forgotten, there was a country called Anywhere. And in the land of Anywhere there was a fine and prosperous city called Anyplace and in an Average Area of the city lived an Upstanding Lady Of Indeterminate Age. Sitting one day in her neat little home, alone as was normal in these later years of hers, she was deafened by the Screaming Silence of a house that used to be so Busy but that was now so Empty. She decided she had to escape this Persistent And Raucous Noise Of Nothingness. She craved the tranquillity of open, green countryside and the wide possibilities of Broad, Bright Blue Skies. She needed a change from the Numbing And Persistent Progression Of Her Silent Days.

Donning a pair of Sensibly Flat Shoes, the Lady Of Indeterminate Age strode decisively out of her house, heading for the hills outside the city: not those made ugly by the gross mansions of the Greedy And Reprehensible One Percent, but those that are Further On And Further Away.

Her journey was long but uneventful, even though it passed through territory known to be plagued by Faeries and Trolls. Not that this concerned our Lady: like Joan Crawford in your world, she had "been around the block" and there were no longer things in This Life that caused her fear. In fact, one Rheumy Old Troll did spot her but, using that Seventh Sense that Trolls have, he decided she was best left undisturbed for he knew, even if she did not, that this was one Lady who had an Appointment With Destiny.

Presently, the Lady came upon the chain of hills she desired to visit. Setting her sights upon the highest hill in the chain, she began to climb. Up and up, and up until the hill levelled off into a wide and peaceful plateau, carpeted in lush green grass, spotted with beautiful wild flowers, and open to the possibilities of the Broad, Bright, Blue Sky.

Setting foot on the plateau, our Lady became aware that a strong Wind was blowing, but it was a pleasant Wind: fierce, powerful but in some way warm and comforting. And as she walked through the Wind, attracted for some reason she could not fathom towards the centre of the lush greenness before her, it seemed to strip away the Everyday Physical Pain of being of An Indeterminate Age and soon it seemed even her Persistently Aching Knees were young and flexible. Our Lady was even sure that, had she had a mirror, she could have held it up to a face that was no longer wrinkled and saggy but firm and unlined, bejewelled with the Bright, Hopeful, Unclouded Eyes Of Youth. Even more remarkably, she was delighted to discover the wind had also succeeded in blowing away the Cobwebs Of Unhappiness And Loneliness that the capriciously malicious Blind Old Weaver that is fate had spun around the Later Years Of Her Life.

Truth be told, upon reaching the middle of the plateau, our Lady felt quite the Giddy Young Girl again.

And just there, in the centre of a green plateau under a Broad, Bright, Blue Sky, she decided to simply stand still and give herself to this Warm And Happy Wind and discover where it would take her.

As she stood, the Wind enfolded her. It wrapped its arms around her and Held Her Tight like her loving and loved husband, dead these ten years gone; a man who had woven a web beneath her, made of love and gossamer thread, to catch her should she fall. It whispered Enjoyable Nonsense in her ears, in the Endlessly Charming Voices Of Children now grown and living lives of their own and it sensuously caressed her breasts and between her legs like the stunningly Handsome Younger Lover she had taken in middle age, who taught her nothing of love but everything of the pleasures of the body. At some points the wind would grow to an intensity that our Lady was sure would knock her down, but then, instead, it would seem to be holding her up: using its own Strange Wisdom, the Wind knew never to blow stronger than she could bear.

The Wind became more and more intense, enfolding and absorbing, filling and possessing her body and mind until it felt to our Lady not like air rushing past her, but her life, played out in thoughts, feelings and emotions, a fast-flowing stream of consciousness. It was Her Story and it was very near its ending. In fact the last few words of the final chapter were being written as she stood here on this windy plateau, under the Broad, Bright, Blue sky. Nothing to regret, nothing to fear. The most natural thing in the world. A beginning, an ending. And another beginning.

Then the Wind reached a new peak of power, stripping away our Lady's shoes and clothes and scattering them across the plateau. It blew the hair from her head, eyebrows and intimate areas, and as it began to peel off her skin in great, loose flaps our Lady had a sense of Coming Apart. She felt no pain, no panic, just a Sense Of Freedom.

Next to go were her eyes, the Wind popping them out of their sockets, the brain following closely behind, squeezing out of the spaces where the eyes had been. Cartilage, muscle and internal organs were the last to be blown away and now our Lady was nothing but a skeleton and a Soul, standing there on an open plateau, and had you also been there you would have been Blinded, for the Soul of the Lady burned with the Brightness Of A Thousand Stars, sitting Incandescent inside her ribcage until the Wind embraced it and carried it up higher and higher, speeding it triumphantly across a Broad, Bright, Blue Sky on a Final Exhilarating, Blissful Journey to That Which Lies Beyond.

Some months later, our Lady's skeleton was discovered; just a pile of old bones, lying atop that isolated plateau. Nobody could be sure to whom these bones had once belonged and it was assumed that they were the Mortal Remains of some Unfortunate Traveller who had been attacked and eaten by Trolls. Thus the Upstanding Lady Of An Indeterminate Age slipped silently and unnoticed into the dense Fog Of Forgotten Stories which makes up so much of history.

And the motto of this tale is: do not fear that which will inevitably seek you out.

Introduction: Floating Away

Walking down the high street, on my way to work,
nothing strange, nothing not normal, just like any other
day
until that pain flares in my chest and in my shoulder
and suddenly I'm falling over.

Flesh and bone hit the pavement, but I'm not there,
I've gone already because today is no ordinary day,
Today is the day I'm floating away.

From above I see myself, lacking in motion, causing a
commotion
amongst the passers-by and I ask myself should I laugh or
cry?
But none of that matters, not today, because today is the
day I'm
floating away.

I stare down my at body, far beneath my dangling feet, I
see just myself,

then the surrounds and roof-tops and then the whole street and

I'm getting higher and higher and soon I'll see the whole city in which

I used to live because today is the day I'm floating away.

This is extra-ordinary, this floating away. I'm sure I should

be scared and shouting and screaming, but this floating away

seems the most natural thing in the world, like I always knew it was

something I would do, that today would be the day that I would float away.

I have a moment of regret because I've not had the chance to say goodbye

to all those who I love and care for (hey, sorry guys, but I had to fly)

but I know, like the soil knows the rain, that we'll meet again because today

is not the first time or the first day that I've floated away.

I didn't always do things right (be that by omission or commission)

or achieve all that I could or should and I didn't always live my best life

and, yes, there was love but also there were harsh words and anger and strife.

But none of that matters, not today, because today is the day I'm floating away.

And I think of the bills and the debt and the struggle to make ends

meet, paying the rent and all the energy spent just to live a life so ordinary and

of all those who said they were my friend but were not, just there for what they got,

and the betrayals and the lies and the precious friend who dies.

But none of that matters, not today, because today is the day I'm floating away.

And I think of the good times, the nights out, the drinks

and the laughing,

the pick-ups, the crafty shags, being young, a good film, a better book, the music

and the dancing, the things I did that worked, the money I had (before I lost it!),

being lucky, knowing what it is to love and be loved,endearments whispered

under the covers, being in a better place than so many others.

But none of that matters, not today, because today is the day that I'm floating away.

And I think of the really shitty stuff of life – the fakes and the freaks and the cheats,

the exploitation, the abuse, the promises made and never kept, all of the times I've

sat and fucking wept, the kids starving in a world of plenty, the privileged son

who's rich before he's twenty, the barbaric cruelty we inflict on animals and each other,

the old and the rich who live off the blood of the poor and the young, the you're too fat, you're too thin, you're too gay, you're too straight, you're too black,

you're too white, you're too left, you're too right - hey, fucker, do you want to fight?

But none of that matters, not today, because today is the day I'm floating away.

I'm leaving it all behind, I'm floating away on this special day. I'm moving faster

now - the street becomes a city, becomes a county, becomes a country, becomes a

continent, becomes a globe and I feel my consciousness explode into light and...

I'm not just me any more...

I'm me, I'm you, I'm a rock, I'm a bird, I'm a flower, I'm an elemental power,

I'm everything and nothing. I'm Alpha and Omega. I am the Universe.

Today I have floated away.

And So it Goes On...

Once upon a time…about now in fact, in a busy and bustling town somewhere on this planet, on the same day and the same time, an old woman lay dying and a baby girl was about to be born.

The old woman felt all that was Familiar and Warm and Known slipping away from her and she felt great fear – she was being drawn down a dark tunnel leading to somewhere she didn't want to go. Powerless to resist she travelled down that tunnel, further and further away from the Known, ever nearer to the Unknown. Her fear grew and grew until before her she suddenly saw a Light At The End Of The Tunnel – and that light seemed so warm and welcoming, exciting and enticing that her fear completely evaporated; the Unknown suddenly seemed so much more exciting and interesting than Known that, instead of resisting her passage down that strange tunnel, she pushed and scrambled her way onwards to the light to emerge, kicking and screaming with hopeful anticipation, into a New Day.

And at the opposite end of that same town…

The baby girl felt all that was Familiar and Warm and Known slipping away from her and she felt great fear – she was being drawn down a dark tunnel leading to somewhere she didn't want to go. Powerless to resist she travelled down that tunnel, further and further away from the Known, ever nearer to the Unknown. Her fear grew and grew until before her she suddenly saw a Light At The End Of The Tunnel – and that light seemed so warm and welcoming, exciting and enticing that her fear completely evaporated; the Unknown suddenly seemed so much more exciting and interesting than Known that, instead of resisting her passage down that strange tunnel, she pushed and scrambled her way onwards to the light to emerge, kicking and screaming with hopeful anticipation, into a New Day.

And so it goes on, and on, and on.....

I hope you enjoyed my little tales...if you did you can read more Tales from Anywhere in my book 'A Curious Book (Dark)' which is available to buy now...to further tempt you here's the first few pages from that book...

The Road To Heaven Passes Through Hell

Part 1. Story.

Once upon a time… many, many years ago in a world long since forgotten, there was a country called Anywhere. And in the land of Anywhere there was a fine and prosperous city called Anyplace and in this fine city lived man who had two children, two boys, brothers born one year apart. For simplicity's sake, let's name the younger brother The Good Brother and the older brother, The Bad Brother.

Now this man was a Wise Man. Not "wise" in the sense of Kindly And Knowledgeable but wise as in the sense of Wise To The Ways Of The World and one of the ways in which he was wise to the ways of the world was that he had come to the understanding, at an early age, that this life (take careful heed of the words 'this life' or this Tale may drown you in despair before you reach its end) rewards not the good but rather those who are selfish and greedy and who take what they want when they want it without regard to the thoughts, feelings or needs of others.

Indeed he had come to the conclusion that Selfishness, Greed and a Lack Of Care for others were the keys to a happy life.

He determined that he would inculcate this philosophy into his two boys.

So again and again throughout the boys' childhood and adolescence the father told his children not to listen to what they were taught at school or elsewhere about Being Nice To Others, or Being Helpful, or Caring…it was all nonsense and would lead to a life of poverty and misery. Instead, he told them, they should be Greedy, Selfish and put their own needs above those of others. There was no Judgement in this World, no Reward for Being Good. Never, he said, think of anybody before you think of yourself, never offer a Hand In Help to another person, never miss a chance to stab someone in the back or kick a man when he was down, never concern yourself with the Feelings Of Others. Take what you want when you want from who you want. Always seek to gain power over others and use that power to hurt and exploit. Never be reluctant to cause damage. This, he said, is the way to Fulfilment And Happiness and a Prosperous and Successful life. When not lecturing the brothers about the wonder of wealth, the rightness of ruthlessness and the prioritization of power he would sprinkle his conversations (such as they were, for his actual interest in them was fairly limited) with the boys with what he considered to be useful 'mottos' such as:

"The value of a man is determined by how much he owns."

"The poor are poor because they are stupid. Punish them for it."

"To satisfy one's own desires at the expense of others is Divine."

"The law does not apply to the rich."

"The tears of others are as balm to your soul."

As a consequence of his philosophy of life the father had, like many bad men before and since, chosen the world of financial dealings as his preferred area of work - buying and selling commodities futures, basic foodstuff to be precise, making much money for himself and other wealthy individuals at the price of poverty and hunger for others. After all, the poor are poor because they are stupid. Punish them for it.

Both brothers listened to the father's oft repeated advice, but not both believed it. The older brother, The Bad Brother, believed and accepted, for he was very much The Son Of The Father, handsome and intelligent, but with an air of callous ruthlessness. Had you met him, you would have felt there was certainly something a bit dark about him, a Touch Of The Troll, as it is said in the lad of Anywhere – that saying being a gross calumny against the Troll race, Trolls, in reality, being gentle and loving creatures unless called upon to protect Goodness and the harmony of the Universal Law Of Equilibrium.

The second brother, The Good Brother thought completely the opposite. He simply could not accept the father's advice; he was more The Son Of The Mother for it was an act of Good Fortune (for the father, not the mother) that the boy's father had, by accident, married a Good Woman. This poor woman he would treat in a truly appalling fashion throughout their married life, humiliating her time and time again with his philandering, lies, abuse, violence and perversions. Whilst handsome and intelligent like the older brother, the younger brother, The Good Brother, had inherited a gentle and caring nature from his mother. Had you met him you would have thought he was a very nice man, though perhaps a bit of a fool (a judgement people come to all too often when they meet a good person).

With the inevitability of the Cycle Of Life, adulthood, as evidenced by the dark hair now sprouting above their top lips, called for the brothers and, at a certain stage, they assumed full manhood (or at least that which society judges to be those things that make a man) and went out Into The World to Build Lives for themselves, The Bad Brother applying the philosophy of the father to all things, The Good Brother rejecting it completely and simply being caring, kind, happy-go-lucky.

And now we come to one of those points in one of my Tales from Anywhere at which you, dear Reader, expect a particular kind of ending. But, as I've said before, this is no fairy tale, this is real life and real life, like nature, is bloody in tooth and claw.

What you want me to say is that after initial success from the application of Ruthlessness And Selfishness The Bad Brother eventually had to pay a price for his wicked ways and ended up poor, alone, a broken man, whilst The Good Brother, after some early struggles, eventually reaped the rewards of his Kindness And Compassion, became rich, married a beautiful woman, had gorgeous children and lived happily ever after.

No. Sorry. That's not how things worked out. This is real life, remember. This is how events really unfolded...and it's a sorry story to tell.

Both brothers went into the world of business. Both

being bright and hardworking, both did well. But The Bad Brother capitalised on his success and, just as the father taught, was Ruthless And Selfish, took what he wanted when he wanted and was happy to tread others into the dirt, to kick a man when he was down, to plunge a knife between the shoulder blades. He became a very, very rich man who was feared if not respected. He married a beautiful woman (who he treated like dirt just as his father had done to his mother), had gorgeous children (in whom he showed some interest but had no real love for), indulged perverse and excessive desires that ruined the lives of The Young and The Innocent. He trod all over people, used, cheated, lied, stole, damaged and raped. And had a fabulous time of it all and lived happily ever after.

The Good Brother, the Kind Compassionate One, never managed to take full advantage of his success in business; he was always thoughtful of the feelings and needs of others and never quite ruthless enough to Take The Necessary Hard Decisions. What's more, being a Kind Fellow, he was always trying to help others who found themselves in difficulty. Seeing such Kindness

And Compassion, people around him (for the reasons we've already established) considered him to be Stupid and Foolish, not a man to be feared or regarded - so they cheated him, used him, stole from him. As a consequence of his Kindness, which others exploited as Weakness, The Good Brother would end up emotionally and financially drained, he would lose his business, his home, his family, his prospects and at the comparatively young age of 43 he would, in despair, end his life by throwing himself from a high window of The Asylum For The Strange And The Different.

And the moral of this particular tale is: The Devil really does have all the best tunes and he absolutely does look after his own.

Or does he?

Now, this is real life, remember…

And maybe I haven't been telling the whole truth?

Maybe I've been acting as journalists do, who in the land of Anywhere (just like in your own world) have long since forgotten that the duty of journalism is to search for the truth and present facts in an unbiased fashion. Instead, journalists long since came under the thrall of The Greedy One Percent (just like in your own world...), prostituting their independence and ability to think critically (or even to think) and confabulating fact and fiction to produce not news but blatant propaganda, always framed in a way that advances whatever the desired agenda of their Greedy One Percent owners/masters/pimps might be.

Maybe I'm an unreliable witness, my independence and credibility undermined by my own wish for money and influence? Maybe I'm a propaganda-peddler, not a truth-teller? Maybe I'm someone who writes for a living; in which case why the heck would you expect me to tell the truth about anything? I mean, come on, making stuff up is what I do!

Part 2. Truth

Here, finally, is the real truth of real life. And it's far from plain and certainly not simple. The version of the bothers' story you have just read is indeed propaganda. It is the one told by The Greedy One Percent to their children as part of their education in how to become effective, society-killing sociopaths ready to assume their natural position in life: ruling over, and living off the blood, sweat and tears of, The Ordinary Folk.

Here is how the life (and death) of the two brothers really unfolded.

Both brothers are indeed exposed to the father's sociopathic philosophy, one does follow it, the other does not.

The Bad Brother does indeed become rich through his lifelong exercise of viciousness, but his world is essentially vacuous and loveless. Despite the trappings of wealth and the Trophy Wife his only real pleasures are the corruption of innocence, the exercise of power to destroy others and a much cherished ability to add to the

Greater Sum Of Misery.

The Good Brother is indeed Kind And Caring. He never becomes rich, but neither does he Want Unduly. Those in life he is kind to do not regard him as a fool, rather as a Good Man. He lives a life full of Love And True Riches.

The Good Brother does not despair, is never incarcerated in The Asylum For The Strange And The Different and does not take his own life.

In fact, both brothers (in a bizarre, synchronicity-laden turn of events such as can only be Spun Together by the Blind Old Weaver Of Fate in her Random, Capricious Sightlessness) died of natural causes on the same day.

And so our story, the real story, begins.

Both brothers, simultaneously - to the very second - knew a sudden, sharp and all-consuming pain, mercifully short-lived, which faded away to darkness, silence, stillness. Then a burning brightness and a sensation of travel, great speed and a sweet freedom as, together, their liberated Souls travelled across the Broad, Bright. Blue Sky to That Which Lies Beyond.

Much to their surprise and bewilderment, the brothers found themselves standing in a strange, never before seen landscape. Under a leaden grey sky, a green landscape of rolling hills, occasionally marked with outcrops of grey rock or patches of thicker, taller vegetation, stretched out as far as the eye could see. Dense patches of fog rolled across the landscape like wearily patrolling soldiers and far, far in the distance rose a hill so high it seemed to be reaching for the grey sky above and atop the hill could clearly be seen a city. And it was a wondrous city, marked with high towers and of achingly beautiful construction. The city gleamed and shone, emitting a light that calmed the mind and lifted the heart. It was a Shining City On Top Of A Hill.

And the brothers turned towards each other. The Good Brother smiled and said, "brother, it's you! I've not seen you in, what, twenty years. It's a delight that we should meet again, but a shame that it's taken death to bring us together…come, let me hold you…" and The Good Brother, being a good person, moved forward with arms open to embrace his brother. But The Bad Brother, bad person that he was, backed away, "mmm, that won't be necessary, thank you, I can't say I know why we're here but I'm sure it's only temporary and I've very much removed myself from old entanglements and I have no wish to get to know you now – what would be the point, you are an Ordinary Person and you have nothing to offer me and you possess nothing I have any interest in." What indeed would be the point? After all, a man's value is determined by what he owns, and The Bad Brother had abandoned The Good Brother two decades back, why, but why, would he want anything to do with a man who owned little, a man of no real value? Ridiculous idea! At this point the situation may have turned embarrassing were it not for a fortuitous interruption in proceedings as a persistent throat clearing sound made both brothers turn around and look behind them.

The source of the throat clearing interruption was standing there. A bored looking, somewhat Ragged And Dyspeptic Angel. "Hullo, Gentlemen," said The Angel, "I'm sorry to interrupt…" at this point The Good Brother explained that that was quite alright, not a problem whilst

The Bad Brother simply scowled at The Angel, which scowling caused The Angel to flap his wings once up and once down in irritation… "but I have some information to impart."

"You may have guessed by now, seeing as you both seem to have at least a modicum of intelligence," continued The Angel "that you have in fact died…for which please accept my congratulations, that whole life business can get terribly tiresome can't it? So, uh, where was I…oh yes…so, you've died and your joyfully liberated souls have sped across a Broad Blue Sky to that which etcetera etcetera…oh dear," the Angel paused, looking infinitely weary, "forgive my lack of enthusiasm, gents…do you know I've being doing this job now for six millennia…day in day out, same old spiel, same old ya-dee-da. Hummph…one would not be an Angel if one did not get a touch bored every now and then, would one?...right, sorry…you've died, okay? You got that bit? Good. Now, contrary to all that silly, religious myth nonsense that you gullible lot down there fall for hook line and sinker, getting to Heaven or, it has to be said, Hell, is not as simple as dying, being judged and ending up in one place or the other. No. Not at all. You see…" at this moment the Angel paused dramatically and then to add to the dramatic effect (for the Angel secretly yearned to be free of being a tour guide for the recently deceased and become an actor) he noisily and pointedly flapped his wings powerfully, once up and once down… "getting to Heaven or Hell is a more of a journey and the road to Heaven passes through…" another dramatic, nay, Shakespearian, pause… "HELL."

By this stage, both brothers were looking a bit concerned and a bit confused, taking in their looks, the Angel realized he still had a bit more explaining to do. "Okay, look, let's get this show on the road. You've both died and you are both, I'm afraid, currently standing in the outer zone of Hell or, as I prefer to call it, the Foothills Of Hell – much more poetic don't you think than 'outer zone'. I do firmly believe that we should all strive, should we not, to ensure that philosophy does not clip the wings of us Angels…" the Angel laughed at his own little pretentious literary allusion… " and over there, the big, big hill in the distance? The one with a Shining City on top? That, my friends is Heaven. That's where you have to journey to, the place you need to reach - if you make the journey successfully then God takes it as proven that you are fit to enter His Kingdom. If you are not successful in your journey, I'm afraid you're doomed to Hell. Now, here comes the important bit, listen carefully. As we three stand here it is, at this time, morning in Hell's Foothills but in a few hours the sun – not that you can see it, the weather here in the Foothills is notoriously grim – the sun will go down and darkness will descend. When that happens, Satan's demons will spill out of Hell proper, trawling it's outer zone for any souls still there who they will drag back with them, down into the bowels of Hell and an eternity of suffering!" This dramatic announcement evinced more drama from the Angel, wings were plumped erect, chin tilted upward and arms thrown skyward.

"So that, gents, should you choose to accept it –ah hah hah hah – is your mission. Now, I suggest you get going while it's still day time. One thing…the Foothills contain certain, er, hazards that may delay or even end your journey, your ability to cope with these hazards would, mmm…might, be much helped if there are people or creatures in Heaven who are prepared to…well…you'll see what I mean. Right, off you go!"

"Can I go with my brother?" asked The Good Brother.

"No, for each man must make his journey through the Foothills of Hell alone. Indeed, it may interest you to know that my Angelic intuition tells me your bother doesn't want to travel with you, anyway…I'm afraid he sees you as a burden, believes he'd do far better on his own. You will go first, your brother will follow later."

"But…but…" stammered The Bad Brother, "I will have less time to make the journey than him, that's not fair!"

"Well, there you go, you shouldn't be thinking bad thoughts in front of an Angel, should you? Take it as your first lesson in the way things work in the Foothills Of Hell."

"You!" exclaimed the Angel, pointing in the direction of The Good Brother, "go now."

And The Good Brother, with one last kind (blanked and ignored) look at his sibling started his attempt to reach Heaven, The Shining City On Top Of A Hill, taking the path that ran through The Foothills of Hell....

What happens next? Buy the book to find out!

Additionally, there's another Tales from Anywhere book, 'A Curious Book (Light)', which is also available to buy now...to further tempt (even more!)you here's the first few pages from that book...

The Boy who was Abandoned in The Asylum for the Strange and the Difficult

Part 1. Mother and Son.

Once upon a time… many, many years ago in a world long since forgotten, there was a country called Anywhere. And in the land of Anywhere there was a fine and prosperous city called Anyplace and in this fine city lived a woman who had three children, two girls and a boy.

Unfortunately for the children The Woman was a person of inordinate selfishness, one of those people who feel that they world revolves around them and them alone, someone who was prepared to do anything to get what she wanted. To make things worse, the children had lost their father at an early age. The poor man had died of a broken heart for during the course of his marriage to The Woman he had come to realise that she had not married him for love but simply as a way of escaping from her own background (which had been rather Poor

And Mean) and gaining Financial Security and Social Standing. For his own reasons, which to this day remain unfathomable, the husband had loved The Woman dearly and simply could not reconcile the love he felt for her with the total lack of love she had for him. So he succumbed to the Sadness Disease (which in your world you call cancer) but beat it to its fatal conclusion by drinking himself to death.

This left three children (another unfathomable that also remains unanswered to this day – exactly why did she have children?) to be raised by one very strange woman. The Woman only had two Real Loves and they were Social Standing and Gambling. She loved nothing more than praise and attention from friends, associates and The Neighbours and, in pursuit of such, would portray herself to those around her as a brave and valiant Single Mother who Devoted Her Life to raising and caring for her darling children, and such performance did indeed bring her much praise and her precious, desired Social Standing.

But The Woman's Truth as she presented it to the world was a Fiction. The Woman's children were left pretty much to bring up themselves, she was an Absent And Unconcerned parent for her love for herself and her needs was too great to spare any love for her children. She put food on the table and clothes on the children's backs but nothing else. And then not always, for almost every cent and penny that came into the household was spent on The Woman's other Great Love: gambling. Oh, how The Woman loved to gamble, for hours and days on end. She would gamble on horses, dogs, rabbits, flashing lights – anything that moved and presented a chance of a chance!

Growing up with this strange, self-obsessed woman was difficult for all three children but most particularly for The Boy. Girls are always cleverer about these things and The Boy's sisters had long since recognised The Mother for the Selfish And Uncaring creature she was and they had simply resolved to get on with life until such time as they were old enough to leave home and never come back. The Boy felt things more keenly for, like his father, he had, for yet another unfathomable reason to this day unexplained, a Deep And Abiding Love for his mother. And he desperately wanted her to return that love, to share a kind word, a warm embrace. Of course, The Woman never did any of these things but the more she showed The Boy that she had no love for him, the more he wanted her to love him and the harder he would try to be loved and he would say:

'Look at this, Mum',

'I love you, Mum',

'Look what we did at school today, Mum.'

'You look nice today, Mum.'

'I made this for you, Mum.'

And The Woman would grunt and turn her back on him and return to her gambling or telling stories to The Neighbours of her sacrifices for her children as a struggling Single Mother.

Truth be told, The Woman didn't just not love her son, she despised him. She saw him as a threat to her Social Standing for whilst The Boy had a pleasing and loving nature and was not unintelligent or untalented (indeed he had a beautiful singing voice) or unattractive, he was small for his fourteen years and had a certain gentle feyness about him – a degree of femininity that she disliked and distrusted. She was very concerned that the child might be a *falulah* (a 'falulah' is Anywhere slang that corresponds to words like 'queer' and 'faggot' in your world).

Now, this Tale is set in some years back in the history of Anywhere, before the brief Golden Age and social, cultural and economic blooming that occurred as a result of breaking the dead grip of The Greedy One Percent (sadly short-lived though that period was) and Social Attitudes were, particularly on matters of difference and sexuality, still very retarded – being identified as a falulah was a matter of great Social Embarrassment and shame and it was widely considered that a person was better off dead than falulah. So- The Mother's suspicions that her son might be 'one of them' caused her considerable concern. Imagine the Social Shame of having a son who was inclined that way. What would the neighbours think? And the damage such shame would cause to her Social Standing! Unacceptable!

Then one day all The Woman's fears were confirmed for The Boy came back from school with a ripped shirt and a bloody lip and tears in his eyes. 'Mum,' he said, 'the other boys beat me and laughed at me and called me a falulah, why mum, why?'

And a spasm of pure terror and shame shot through The Woman. See, she had been right, the boy was a fulalah and now other people were beginning to notice! Oh, the shame, all those years of building up her Social Standing were going to be ruined by this horrible, useless falulah child.

'Well, I'm not surprised,' said the infuriated mother, 'I mean look at you, you're pathetic, you're so small, you're tiny compared to the other boys and you sound like a girl. Huh, they're right you are a falulah!' With these words she walked towards her child and The Boy, despite her harsh words, thought (or at least fervently hoped) that she was going to comfort him. Instead she stopped short of The Boy, raised a hand above her head and slammed it down with all her strength across his face, knocking him to the floor. 'Get upstairs to your room!'

she screamed. And as the terrified child did just that, she screamed after him:

'Dwarf!'

'Midget!'

'Falulah!'

'Falulah!'

Calming herself, The Mother thought about what she should do. A falulah for a son, what a humiliation. She couldn't let this miserable child threaten her Social Standing – but short of murdering the child (which, to be quite frank, she would have done were it not for the fear of being caught) what could be done? And she thought. And she thought. And she thought. And she came up with a plan.

The next day, whilst The Boy was at school, she made her way to The Asylum For The Strange And The Different.

Part 2. The Asylum For The Strange And The Different.

To understand what happened next in this tale it is necessary to understand about The Asylum For The Strange And The Different and its position in Anywhere's society at this point in Anywhere's history. Fundamentally, it was a dumping ground – for The Strange and The Different – The Strange being those considered to be mad and The Different being those who didn't quite fit in with society because they perhaps had strange views and ideas, or whose politics were regarded as dangerous or who were, perhaps, falulahs.

Once an unfortunate individual was placed in The Asylum, that was it, They were gone. Lost. Invisible. Never to be heard from again. No inmates of The Asylum ever left that grim place alive.

And The Asylum was truly dreadful, a black pit of madness and despair: those who worked there only worked there as a very last resort, out of desperation to earn some kind of living. Faeries would not fly within a two mile radius of it and Trolls would not even mention it in conversation (to do so was considered to bring the worst of luck): even Death was a reluctant to go there, though The Devil did think it rather a fun place to visit.

Certainly nobody ever came to see anybody at The Asylum; after all it was where Strange or Difficult were dumped and why, having got rid of them, would one want to visit them?

Within the walls of The Asylum there was no concept of treatment or care for its reluctant inmates. The Different were there simply to keep their disturbing ideas and proclivities away from wider society – that was all, nothing to do but keep them locked away until they died. The Different – they were just mad and there was nothing to done about that: in the land of Anywhere at this time madness was considered not be an illness or dysfunction but an Altered State. The belief was that mad people were mad because they had, in some way, communed with The Devil. During the course of their congress with Satan, he had allowed them to open the pages of his Book Of The Dead. The Devil's Book Of The Dead is a kind of Satanic Stamp Album. An album of huge size and length in which The Devil, the Ultimate Connoisseur Of Suffering, records (for his delight and delectation) the saddest of deaths – those being to The Devil (and to your narrator) the premature deaths, be it by disease or violence, of The

Young And The Innocent. And each death is recorded not in words, instead it is written in emotion, in the pain and sadness that was endured in the course of that death. As such, The Devil's Book Of Death contains a depth of pain so great, so deep, so profound that to open even one page for one second is enough to plunge any man or woman into madness, a madness that is pure and unchangeable – an Altered State. All that is to be done with a person who has peered into The Devil's Book Of Death is to assign them until death to The Asylum For The Strange And The Different.

So, there you have it, The Asylum For The Strange And The Different was no more or no less than a place where those considered mad, different, awkward or embarrassing were sent to die. Once in, there was no way out except death. To be an inmate in The Asylum was to 'live' in a state of non-existence.

Let's return now to my little tale. Having been informed of the nature and purpose of The Asylum For The Strange And The Different you've probably guessed the purpose of The Mother's visit there. That's right, she'd gone there to visit the Director of The Asylum to plead her case for having The Boy admitted (dumped and forgotten until death) there. All in all, things went well for her. The Director, a miserable bigot of a man who abhorred difference of any kind and particularly falulahs, had agreed with her. Her case was justified, keeping a falulah in the family home would indeed result in Unacceptable Embarrassment to her with a concomitant drop in her Social Status. However, just to oil the wheels, smooth the path and get The Boy admitted the next day might she consider a Small Token Of Her Appreciation, maybe just lie back and lift up her skirt, just twenty minutes of her time?

The Mother considered the Director's request to have sex with her and thought, why not if it's going to get the job done and get that horrible child out my life? The decision was made all the easier to make because on the way to The Asylum she had suddenly realised another 'plus' of getting rid of The Boy: one less mouth to feed would mean more money for one of the true loves of her life – gambling! Don't be shocked, I did tell you she was a truly awful woman...

The next day, The Boy was getting ready for school (The Boy and his sister's always got themselves ready for school, The Mother never being awake that early in the day due to having been up late gambling) when, much to his surprise his mother appeared, fully dressed, bright and smiling.

'Well hullo, my little man!' she said cheerily, 'and how are you today? My son, my beloved son, you've been having a difficult time so today there'll be no school – you're coming to the shops with me and we're going to buy you a treat and then we'll go for a lovely Sludge burger!'

And The Boy beamed from ear to ear, for this was Heaven to him, at last his mother was being nice to him, the only thing he really, really wanted in life was finally coming to pass!

The Boy and his mother jumped into a clarb (the Anywhere equivalent of a London black cab) and began their journey. The Mother explained to The Boy that before they went to the shops she just had to stop off somewhere and 'pick something up for a friend.' The Boy nodded and smiled and took hold of his mother's hand and squeezed it gently. This vaguely repulsed The Mother but she accepted it, even squeezed The Boy's hand gently back – keep the horrible little thing happy and quiet, she thought, I'll soon be rid of it, she thought.

By and by, the clarb came to, you've guessed it, The Asylum For The Strange And The Difficult, and the mother said 'come on, little man, come with me – this thing I have to collect is quite heavy so you can give me a hand!'

Willingly The Boy jumped out of the clarb with his mother, happy to help. Seeing the huge, grey, bleak, hulking building before him he felt a sense of doom and despair but comforted himself with the thought that he was with his mother, she'd make sure that everything was fine.

Into The Asylum went mother and soon. Down long, depressing corridors painted that sickly, pale shade of green beloved by bureaucracies in all worlds everywhere, until they came to a blank, anonymous looking door. 'Ah, yes,' said the mother, 'this is where we should be – be a dear and pop into this room will you and pick up the package there…' and she swung open that anonymous door. And The Boy, eager to please, entered the room and before he could register the fact that it contained no package, two burly Asylum employees threw a thick, heavy net over him and wrestled him to the ground, dragging him out of the room and down, down, down another long, depressing corridor and as he kicked and screamed and was hauled away to a state of non-existence oh, how the mother laughed and she shouted:

'Idiot!'

'Midget!'

'Girl!'

'Falulah!'

'Falulah!'

And The Boy cried:

'Mummy!'

'No, mummy, no!'

'Why, mummy?'

'Why?'

'Why….'

What happens next? Buy the book and find out!

Also by the same author and available to buy now:
I Really, Really Want It. A Novel.

"Excellent writing. Fresh, engaging and pushing the boundaries. It's written by someone who has obviously worked in the celebrity industry he describes and provides a fascinating left-field insight into a glamorous but tawdry world." U.S. REVIEWS

Celebrities have secrets. Meet the man who knows them all and will do anything to keep them quiet. Even murder.

Andrew Manning has spent 20 years masterfully reviving celebrity careers that have been rocked by scandal, but now some particularly difficult and demanding characters are about strain even his abilities to the limit:

Shelley. Model and fashion icon, she's determined to blackmail her closeted, gay footballer husband into a lucrative divorce settlement...but Shelley has her own dark   secret.

Joey. Handsome, young reality TV star and sex symbol. His career is in tatters after launching an expletive-laden attack against the Queen of England, but he's determined to hang on to his celebrity even if it means slowly poisoning himself to death.

The Producer, a king in the world of entertainment - rich, powerful, sexually deviant and a serial abuser of hopeful young wannabes.

Charlie. Morbidly obese, murderous Mafiosi adviser (and creature) to...

Janey. Musical superstar, mad, bad and dangerous to know. Janey consumes liquidized human fetuses to preserve her youthful (or should that be vampiric?) good looks.

Johnny. Andrew's partner, a psychopath with a heart of gold and voices in his head. He's on a mission to murder as many celebrities as possible.

And when an ambitious young photographer snaps Janey in the middle of one of her disgusting meals, things begin to spin rapidly out of control for Andrew.

How will Andrew reconcile the demands of such disparate and desperate characters. And who's going to end up dead?

'I Really Really Want It' also features shocking cameo performances from a glittering list of famous, household names. Is your favourite celebrity in the book?

"A close look into the seemingly insane experiences of celebrities….captivating and unique...recommended."

U.S. REVIEWS

Printed in Great Britain
by Amazon